To D.A., fellow writer and E.H., opera-loving granddaughter.

— Ellie Alldredge-Bell

Also by Ellie Alldredge-Bell:
Sitting on a Zinnia, Little Creek Press, 2012

The illustrations in this book were painted in oils on cotton rag paper.

Library of Congress Cataloging-in-Publication Data

Alldredge-Bell, Ellie.
Luigi at the Opera / Ellie Alldredge-Bell, illustrated by Stacey Williams-Ng. — 1st ed.

p. cm.

Summary: A boy visits the opera with his grandfather.
ISBN 978-0-9896688-2-8

[1. Opera — Fiction. 2. Juvenile Opera.] I. Title.

Dewey class no. [E]
2014937706

LITTLE
BAHALIA
PUBLISHING

2625 S. Greeley St., Suite 130
Milwaukee, WI 53207

LUIGI
at the
Opera

Luigi loves opera.

He listens to people singing stories in Grandpa's car.

Happy stories. Funny stories. Sad stories.

"We're opera aficionados," says Grandpa Rigoletto. "Opera lovers."

Luigi loves going to the opera with Grandpa Rigoletto.

Today they are going to see an opera about a ghost ship.

Grandpa Rigoletto wears a tuxedo and Luigi wears a bow tie.

"I am a ghost pirate, Grandpa!" His opera glasses are just like pirate eye patches.

Inside the opera house, Luigi and Grandpa Rigoletto stop and look up.

Chandeliers—gold, glittering lights.

"Magnifico my nipote," says Grandpa Rigoletto.

"Awesome," says Luigi.

At the door of the theatre, an usher hands them a program.

Each row has a letter, and each seat a number.

"Find our seats," says Grandpa Rigoletto.

"I hope you are big enough to hold it down!"

The auditorium lights go out.

Quiet.

The musicians in the orchestra
pit seem close when Luigi uses his
opera glasses.

The piccolo player scratches her nose
with the piccolo.

The director lifts his baton.

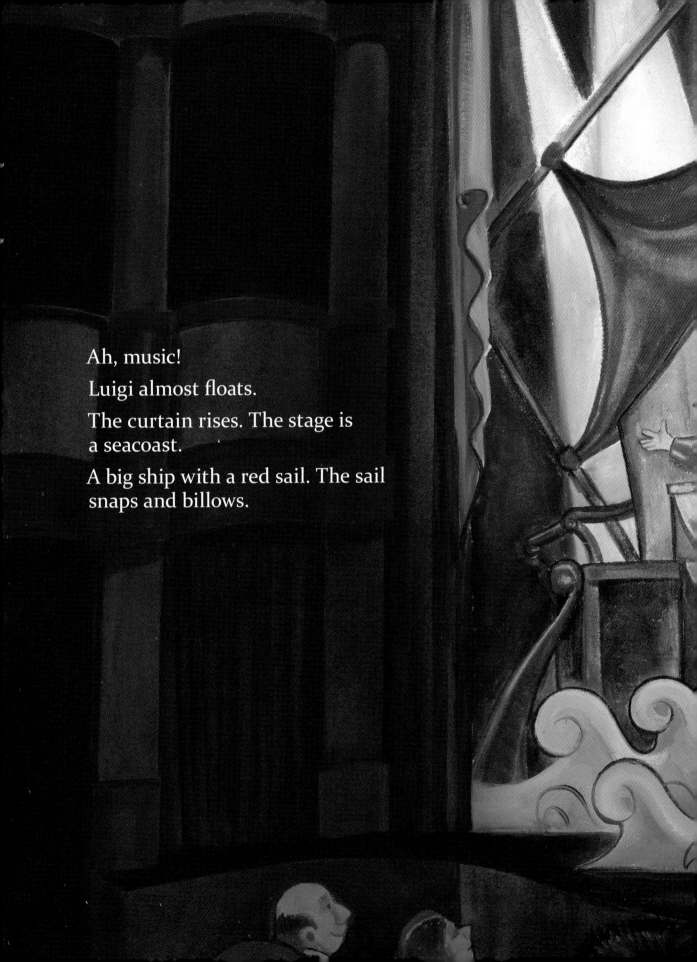

Ah, music!

Luigi almost floats.

The curtain rises. The stage is
a seacoast.

A big ship with a red sail. The sail
snaps and billows.

During intermission, Luigi and Grandpa Rigoletto go to the lobby for a snack.

Luigi munches a biscotti.

Grandpa Rigoletto drinks champagne.

Lights flicker. It is time for the rest of the opera.

The curtain rises. The storm is over, and the ship is gone.

A beautiful woman with big hair sings with the violins.

Suddenly a lady in the row
begins to cough.

Cough.

Cough.

"Shhhhh," people whisper. "Quiet."

Luigi reaches into his pocket.

"Thanks," whispers the smiling lady.

Luigi hears a snore.

Grandpa Rigoletto's head nods toward his cummerbund.

Luigi gives him a little nudge.

"Wake up."

Grandpa Rigoletto opens his eyes.

"Just listening, my aficionado." Grandpa Rigoletto smiles.

The opera ends.
Everyone claps.
"Bravo," someone yells.

"Bravo," booms Grandpa Rigoletto.

"Bravo," echoes Luigi.

The curtain opens and the cast bows.

The audience stands and keeps on clapping.

Outside the opera house, Grandpa Rigoletto and Luigi stroll down the avenue.

"Thank you for escorting me to the opera," says Grandpa Rigoletto.

"I loved it," said Luigi.

"We are true opera aficionados, Grandpa Rigoletto," said Luigi.

"Opera lovers!" say Grandpa Rigoletto and Luigi together.

La Fine

"the End"

About the Opera in this Book

The real-life opera that Luigi and his Grandpa visit in this story is called "The Flying Dutchman." It was written over 150 years ago by a German composer named Richard Wagner.

When the opera begins, we see a ship lost in a violent storm at sea. The ship's captain is named Daland, and he soon drops anchor next to another ship, which has ghost pirates on it! We soon find out that the pirate captain has been cursed to sail the oceans of the earth forever. As part of his curse, he is allowed to come onto land once every seven years, and his goal is to find a woman who will fall in love with him. If he can find true love, the curse will be broken.

Daland greets the Dutchman. He does not know that the Dutchman is a ghost pirate. The Dutchman tells Daland that he will give the captain all the treasures aboard his ship if Daland will let him marry his daughter.

You'll have to go see the opera to find out what happens next! Do you think Daland's daughter Senta will fall in love with a ghost

Words to know...

aficionado: Sounds like "a-FISH-eeya-nah-dough." This is an Italian word for someone who really likes something. Luigi really likes opera, so he is an *aficionado*.

biscotti: A kind of cookie.

chandeliers: These are very fancy light fixtures, often made of crystal or sparkling glass.

cummerbund: A wide belt that is worn with a gentleman's tuxedo, for decoration. It is often made of satin or silk.

intermission: This is the halfway point in an opera or play when everyone takes a break, like recess.

nipote: The Italian word for "grandson" or "nephew." This is what Grandpa calls Luigi.

piccolo: This is an Italian word, pronounced "PEE-colo." It means "little," and in the orchestra,